W9-BVG-762

The Perfect Gift

DISCARD

Henry Lily Mei Pablo Padma

by Paula Yoo

illustrated by Shirley Ng-Benitez

Lee & Low Books Inc. New York

To my "perfect gifts"—my cousins' kids: Nate, Adeline, Julia, Noah, Evelyn, Lauren, Josiah, Faith, and Elijah!—P.Y.

With love to my dear baby brother, Doug—S.N-B.

LEE & LOW BOOKS Inc., 95 Madison Avenue, New York, NY 10016
leeandlow.com
Book design by Maria Mercado
Book production by The Kids at Our House
The illustrations are rendered in watercolor and altered digitally
Manufactured in China by Imago
Printed on paper from responsible sources
(hc) 10 9 8 7 6 5 4 3 2 1
(pb) 10 9 8 7 6 5 4 3 2 1
First Edition
Library of Congress Cataloging-in-Publication Data
Names: Yoo, Paula, author. | Ng-Benitez, Shirley, illustrator.
Title: The perfect gift / by Paula Yoo; illustrated by Shirley Ng-Benitez.
Description: First edition. | New York: Lee & Low Books Inc., [2018]
Series: [Dive into reading; 5] | Summary: As her baby brother's 100-day celebration approaches, Mei struggles to find the perfect gift for him. Includes directions for making traditional red eggs.
Identifiers: LCCN 2017035215 | ISBN 9781620145678 (hardcover: alk. paper)
 ISBN 9781620145685 (pbk.: alk. paper)
Subjects: | CYAC: Birthdays—Fiction. | Gifts—Fiction. | Brothers and sisters—Fiction. | Babies—Fiction. | Chinese Americans—Fiction. | Family life—Fiction.
Classification: LCC PZ7.Y8156 Per 2018 | DDC [E]--dc23
LC record available at https://lccn.loc.gov/2017035215

Contents

Red Eggs

Mei loved her baby brother, Ming.
She liked to draw pictures of him.

Soon Ming would be 100 days old.
There would be a big party for Ming.

Grandma came to help.
She brought many eggs.
"Are you going to bake a cake?"
asked Mei.

"No," said Grandma.
"We will color the eggs red
for good luck.
We will give the eggs
to our guests."

Mei helped Grandma color
the eggs red.
"Now we have lots of
good luck!" said Mei.

Mei's mom gave her red cards.
"You may invite your friends
to the party," said Mei's mom.

Toy Store

Mei saw her friends
Henry, Lily, Pablo, and Padma.

"We are having a big party for Ming," said Mei.
"You are all invited to the party."
"Cool!" said Padma.

"I don't know what
to give Ming," said Mei.
"I want my gift to be perfect."

"What toys does he like?"
asked Lily.
"I don't know," said Mei.
"He likes to sleep a lot."

"How about a truck?"
asked Padma.
"Boys like trucks."

"I don't like trucks,"
said Henry.
"I like to play music.
How about a drum?"
"I don't think my mom
will like that," said Mei.

"Let's go to the toy store,"
said Pablo.
"You can find
the perfect gift there."
"That's a good idea,"
said Mei.

"I'll ask my dad to take us,"
said Pablo.
They all walked to the toy store.

They looked at the toys.
"What will you get for Ming?"
asked Lily.
"I don't know," said Mei.
"Toys cost a lot of money."

Mei went home without a gift.

The Perfect Gift

It was the morning of the party.
Mei's dad cleaned all the rooms.
Mei's mom cooked all the food.

Grandma dressed Ming
in a red shirt and pants.

Mei was sad.
"Why are you sad?"
asked Grandma.

"I don't have a gift for Ming,"
said Mei.
"I wanted to find the perfect gift."
"The perfect gift comes
from the heart," said Grandma.

Mei went to her room.
She looked at all her toys.
She did not want to give
Ming an old toy.

Mei saw her drawings of Ming.
Mei had an idea.
She would make a book
of her drawings for Ming.

It was time for the party.
Mei's mom and dad carried Ming
around the room.
Everyone hugged Ming.

Mei and Grandma gave everyone
red eggs for good luck.

It was time for the gifts.
"Happy 100 days," said Mei.
"I made a book for you."

Ming smiled.
"Ming loves your gift,"
said Mei's dad.

Grandma hugged Mei.
"You found the perfect gift,"
said Grandma.
"It's perfect because it came
from my heart," said Mei.

Mei loved sharing the book
with Ming.

☆ **Activity** ☆

In Chinese culture, some families celebrate a baby's first 100 days. It is traditional for the family to give red eggs to guests. The egg symbolizes good luck and unity. Here is how to make red eggs:

1. Place eggs in a saucepan filled with cold water.
2. With the help of an adult, turn on the stove and heat the water to a boil.
3. Once the water is boiling, lower the heat to let the eggs simmer.
4. Simmer the eggs for at least 12 to 15 minutes until they are hard-boiled.
5. Take the eggs out of the pan with a slotted spoon and place them in a bowl. Run cold water over the eggs to cool them.
6. Once the eggs are cool enough to handle, dip each egg into a bowl of food-safe red dye with a slotted spoon.
7. Let the eggs dry on a paper towel.
8. Place the red eggs in a festive bowl for your guests to enjoy!